Rosa Alchemica, The Tables of the Law & The Adoration of the Magi

By William Butler Yeats

ISBN: 978-1-63118-421-5

Esoteric Classics:
Occult Fiction

Other Books in this Series and Related Titles

The Devil in Love by Jacques Cazotte (978–1–63118–499–4)

A Weird Tale & Other Supernatural Stories by W Q Judge (978–1–63118–518–2)

Confessions of an English Opium–Eater by T De Quincey (978–1–63118–485–7)

On the Cave of the Nymphs in the Odyssey by Thomas Taylor (978-1-63118-505-2)

Rosicrucian Rules, Secret Signs, Codes and Symbols by various (978–1–63118–488–8)

The Janeites, The Man Who Would Be King and Other Stories of Freemasonry by Rudyard Kipling (978–1–63118–480–2)

The Treasure of Atlantis by J Allan Dunn (978-1-63118-522-9)

The Poem of Hashish by A Crowley & C Baudelaire (978-1-63118-484-0)

The Great God Pan by Arthur Machen (978–1–63118–528–1)

The Star and the Garter by Aleister Crowley (978-1-63118-406-2)

Hermetic Arcanum by Jean d'Espagnet (978-1-63118-519-9)

Thirty–One Hymns to the Star Goddess by Frater Achad (978–1–63118–422–2)

A Collection of Magical Writings, Fiction, Poetry & Essays by Aleister Crowley (978–63118–424–6)

With the Adepts or An Adventure Among the Rosicrucians (978-1-63118-523-6)

The Sword of Welleran and Other Stories by Lord Dunsany (978-1-63118-501-4)

The Smoky God or A Voyage to the Inner World by Emerson (978-1-63118-423-9)

The Inmost Light and Other Tales by Arthur Machen (978–1–63118–531–1)

A Collection of Fiction and Essays by Occult Writers on Supernatural and Metaphysical Subjects by various (978–1–63118–510–6)

The A. E. Waite Reader: A Selection of Occult Essays (978–1–63118–515–1)

The Leadbeater Reader: A Selection of Occult Essays (978–1–63118–483–3)

Audio versions are also available on Audible, Amazon and Apple

Other Books in this Series and Related Titles

Paracelsus, the Four Elements and Their Spirits by M P Hall (978-1-63118-400-0)

The Magician's Heavenly Chaos by Thomas Vaughan (978-1-63118-500-7)

Masonic and Rosicrucian History by M P Hall & H Voorhis (978-1-63118-486-4)

Tao Te Ching & Commentary by Lao Tzu & C Johnston (978-1-63118-495-6)

The Influence of Pythagoras on Freemasonry and Other Essays (978-1-63118-404-8)

The Golden Verses of Pythagoras: Five Translations (978-1-63118-479-6)

On the Philadelphian Gold by Philochrysus & Philadelphus (978-1-63118-511-3)

The Secret Book of the Philosopher's Stone by Artephius (978-1-63118-517-5)

Aurora of the Philosophers by Paracelsus (978-1-63118-507-6)

A Collection of Early Writings on Astral Travel (978-1-63118-477-2)

The Ceremony of Initiation: Analysis & Commentary (978-1-63118-473-4)

The Old Past Master by Carl H Claudy (978-1-63118-464-2)

The Path of Light: A Manual of Maha-Yana Buddhism (978-1-63118-471-0)

The Hymns of Hermes by G. R. S. Mead (978-1-63118-405-5)

Clairvoyance and Psychic Abilities by Leadbeater & Besant (978-1-63118-403-1)

Catholicism, Yoga and Hinduism by Hartmann &c (978-1-63118-478-9)

The Feminine Occult by various authors (978-1-63118-711-7)

Ancient Mysteries and Secret Societies by M P Hall (978-1-63118-410-9)

*A Collection of Writings Related to Occult, Esoteric, Rosicrucian and Hermetic Literature,
Including Freemasonry, the Kabbalah, the Tarot, Alchemy and Theosophy*
various authors *Volumes 1-4*
(978-1-63118-713-1) (978-1-63118-714-8)
(978-1-63118-715-5) (978-1-63118-716-2)

Audio Versions are also available on Audible, Amazon and Apple

Table of Contents

INTRODUCTION

The word "esoteric" can be difficult to define. Esotericism in general can be seen less as a system of beliefs and more as a category, which encompasses numerous, different systems of beliefs. It's a bit of juxtaposition, since the word "esoteric" indicates something that few people know about, while the term itself broadly covers numerous philosophies, practices, areas of study and belief systems.

In a greater sense, Esotericism acts as a storehouse for secret knowledge, which is often considered ancient (by *tradition, if not by fact*), passed down from generation to generation, in private. At various times in history, simply possessing the knowledge of some of these subjects, was considered illegal and a jailable offence, if discovered. This usually included such general topics as Alchemy, Pharmacology, Qabalah, Hermeticism, Occultism, Ceremonial Magic, Astrology, Divination, Rosicrucianism and so on. Collectively, these areas of study were often referred to as the esoteric sciences.

Sometimes, the outer garment of a subject isn't esoteric, while what is hidden beneath it, is. As an example, Freemasonry isn't necessarily esoteric by nature (at *least not anymore*), but certain signs, passwords and handshakes given to the candidate during their initiation, are in fact, esoteric, in the sense that they are hidden from the general public.

Today, in the twenty-first century, such topics are readily available at bookstores across the country, and numerous main-steam publishers offer beginners guides and coffee-table volumes on many of these subjects, intended for mass appeal. Books like *"The Secret"* have turned previously arcane topics into household knowledge. All that being the case, however, it isn't to say that there still aren't buried secrets to uncover, ancient wisdom being ignored and forgotten mysteries to be explored. In fact, it is often that we are only able to further our own studies by standing on the shoulders of these disappearing giants.

Lamp of Trismegistus is doing its part to help preserve humanity's esoteric history by making some of these classics available to those students who are seeking to unearth the knowledge of these ancient colossi.

So, be sure to check other titles from our *Esoteric Classics* series, as well as our *Occult Fiction*, *Theosophical Classics*, *Foundations of Freemasonry Series*, *Supernatural Fiction*, *Paranormal Research Series*, *Studies in Buddhism* and our *Christian Apocrypha Series*. You can also download the audio versions of most of these titles from Amazon, Apple or Audible, for learning on the go.

PREFACE

From an early age, Yeats showed an interest in occult topics, which no doubt led to the creation of the Hermetic Society in Dublin, in the mid 1880's, a group which he founded and presided over. His organization caught the eye of Madame Blavatsky, who personally invited him to join the Theosophical Society, a year later. Once a member, he quickly received an invitation to join the ranks of the society's inner-order collective, the Esoteric Section. A year later still, he would join the Hermetic Order of the Golden Dawn in their formative years, taking the magical motto *"Demon Est Deus Inversus."* However, perhaps as a result of this newly acquired membership, the Theosophical Society would end up expelling him from their ranks, soon thereafter.

It was during this general time of esoteric memberships, though several years after he had settled into a routine of it all, that Yeats wrote the following three tales. And, one can tell from reading the first and earliest piece, *Rosa Alchemica*, that Yeats was still caught up in the imagined ideal of what recruitment into a selective, initiatory occult organization might be like. The descriptions found in *Rosa Alchemica* are fanciful and mysterious. Ultimately, they are much different than his actual and more mundane experiences that he encountered in the Theosophical Society the Hermetic Order of the Golden Dawn.

Still, it's obvious from the descriptions and narration that Yeats continued to maintain a love for the idealized intent behind the oral tradition of these societies, even if the reality of it all usually turned out to be a disappointing, mystical book club.

Various critics over the decades, including some contemporaneous to Yeats, have labeled these stories difficult to understand; however, these same critics were never his intended audience. These critics weren't interested in or versed with an understanding of occult imagery and vocabulary, which is who Yeats was imagining his reader to be.

In contrast, the readers approaching these stories with a base knowledge of alchemical terms and magical ideas, perhaps even those who share the same passion that Yeats held for uncovering the secrets of the Great Work, certainly walk away with a better general impression of them.

Yeats scholar Brady Peneton has this to say, regarding the trilogy of stories, "The alchemical tradition refers to the magical tradition of reshaping the psychology of oneself or another person using literature, symbol, meditation, altered states of consciousness, and other related techniques. For Yeats, poetry and drama were also forms of magic, much like ritual, invocation, or other occult practices in which formless entities are given form."

All three stories feature the character of Michael Robartes (as well as the character of Owen Aherne in the second two tales), and though it may seem obvious that it's this character that connects all of these tales, what really connects them all is Yeats imagining the hidden fraternity of old tradition which he longed for initiation into. Instead, Yeats spent much of his life seeking for and being disappointed by the mystical ideal, the hidden secrets and promises of ascended masters that were offered to the select few, the initiated, but ultimately always out of reach. Yeats sought entrance into a mythical life that never ceased to elude him, and these three stories are but one example he left behind, of that search.

In the years to come, this is a theme that Yeats would return to, time and time again, as he continued to search for something bigger than himself, something beyond this mortal coil that binds all of us to this plane on Earth; a plane that he ultimately was never able transcend.

ROSA ALCHEMICA

Part I

O blessed and happy he, who knowing the mysteries of the gods, sanctifies his life, and purifies his soul, celebrating orgies in the mountains with holy purifications. -*Euripides.*

It is now more than ten years since I met, for the last time, Michael Robartes, and for the first time and the last time his friends and fellow students; and witnessed his and their tragic end, and endured those strange experiences, which have changed me so that my writings have grown less popular and less intelligible, and driven me almost to the verge of taking the habit of St. Dominic. I had just published *Rosa Alchemica*, a little work on the Alchemists, somewhat in the manner of Sir Thomas Browne, and had received many letters from believers in the arcane sciences, upbraiding what they called my timidity, for they could not believe so evident sympathy but the sympathy of the artist, which is half pity, for everything which has moved men's hearts in any age. I had discovered, early in my researches, that their doctrine was no merely chemical phantasy, but a philosophy they applied to the world, to the elements and to man himself; and that they sought to fashion gold out of common metals merely as part of an universal transmutation of all things into some divine and imperishable substance; and this enabled me to make my little book a fanciful reverie over the transmutation of life into art, and a cry of measureless desire for a world made wholly of essences.

I was sitting dreaming of what I had written, in my house in one of the old parts of Dublin; a house my ancestors had made almost famous through their part in the politics of the city and their friendships with the famous men of their generations; and was feeling an unwonted happiness at having at last accomplished a long—cherished design, and made my rooms an expression of this favourite doctrine. The portraits, of more historical than artistic interest, had gone; and tapestry, full of the blue and bronze of peacocks, fell over the doors, and shut out all history and activity untouched with beauty and peace; and now when I looked at my Crevelli and pondered on the rose in the hand of the Virgin, wherein the form was so delicate and precise that it seemed more like a thought than a flower, or at the grey dawn and rapturous faces of my Francesca, I knew all a Christian's ecstasy without his slavery to rule and custom; when I pondered over the antique bronze gods and goddesses, which I had mortgaged my house to buy, I had all a pagan's delight in various beauty and without his terror at sleepless destiny and his labour with many sacrifices; and I had only to go to my bookshelf, where every book was bound in leather, stamped with intricate ornament, and of a carefully chosen colour: Shakespeare in the orange of the glory of the world, Dante in the dull red of his anger, Milton in the blue grey of his formal calm; and I could experience what I would of human passions without their bitterness and without satiety. I had gathered about me all gods because I believed in none, and experienced every pleasure because I gave myself to none, but held myself apart, individual, indissoluble, a mirror of polished steel: I looked in the triumph of this imagination at the birds of Hera, glowing in the firelight as though they were wrought of jewels; and to my mind, for which symbolism was a necessity, they seemed the doorkeepers of my world, shutting out all that was not of as affluent a beauty as their own; and for a moment I thought as I had thought in so many other moments, that it was possible to rob life of every bitterness except the bitterness of death; and then a thought which had followed this thought, time after time, filled me with a passionate sorrow. All those forms: that Madonna with her brooding purity, those rapturous faces singing in the morning light, those bronze divinities with their passionless dignity, those wild shapes rushing from despair to despair, belonged to a divine world wherein I had no part; and every experience, however profound, every perception, however exquisite, would bring me the bitter dream of a limitless energy I could never know, and even in my most perfect moment I would be two selves, the one watching with heavy eyes the other's moment of content. I had heaped about me the gold born in the crucibles of others; but the supreme dream of the alchemist, the transmutation of the weary heart into a weariless spirit, was as far from me as, I doubted not, it had been from him also. I turned to my last purchase, a set of alchemical apparatus which, the dealer in the Rue le Peletier had assured me, once belonged to Raymond Lully, and as I joined the *alembic* to the *athanor* and laid the *lavacrum maris* at their side, I understood the alchemical doctrine, that all beings, divided from the great deep where spirits wander, one and yet a multitude, are weary; and sympathized, in the pride of my connoisseurship, with the consuming thirst for destruction which made the alchemist veil under his symbols of lions and dragons, of eagles and ravens, of dew and of nitre, a search for an essence which would dissolve all mortal things. I repeated to myself the ninth key of Basilius Valentinus, in which he compares the fire of the last day to the fire of the alchemist, and the world to the alchemist's furnace, and would have us know that all must be dissolved before the divine substance, material gold or immaterial ecstasy, awake. I had dissolved indeed the mortal world and lived amid immortal essences, but had obtained no miraculous ecstasy. As I thought of these things, I drew aside the curtains and looked out into the darkness, and it seemed to my troubled fancy that all those little points of light filling the sky were the furnaces of innumerable divine alchemists, who labour continually, turning lead into gold, weariness into ecstasy, bodies into souls, the darkness into God; and at their perfect labour my mortality grew heavy, and I cried out, as so many dreamers and men of letters in our age have cried, for the birth of that elaborate spiritual beauty which could alone uplift souls weighted with so many dreams.

Part II

My reverie was broken by a loud knocking at the door, and I wondered the more at this because I had no visitors, and had bid my servants do all things silently, lest they broke the dream of my inner life. Feeling a little curious, I resolved to go to the door myself, and, taking one of the silver candlesticks from the mantlepiece, began to descend the stairs. The servants appeared to be out, for though the sound poured through every corner and crevice of the house there was no stir in the lower rooms. I remembered that because my needs were so few, my part in life so little, they had begun to come and go as they would, often leaving me alone for hours. The emptiness and silence of a world from which I had driven everything but dreams suddenly overwhelmed me, and I shuddered as I drew the bolt. I found before me Michael Robartes, whom I had not seen for years, and whose wild red hair, fierce eyes, sensitive, tremulous lips and rough clothes, made him look now, just as they used to do fifteen years before, something between a debauchee, a saint, and a peasant. He had recently come to Ireland, he said, and wished to see me on a matter of importance: indeed, the only matter of importance for him and for me. His voice brought up before me our student years in Paris, and remembering the magnetic power he had once possessed over me, a little fear mingled with much annoyance at this irrelevant intrusion, as I led the way up the wide staircase, where Swift had passed joking and railing, and Curran telling stories and quoting Greek, in simpler days, before men's minds, subtilized and complicated by the romantic movement in art and literature, began to tremble on the verge of some unimagined revelation. I felt that my hand shook, and saw that the light of the candle wavered and quivered more than it need have upon the Maenads on the old French panels, making them look like the first beings slowly shaping in the formless and void darkness. When the door had closed, and the peacock curtain, glimmering like many— coloured flame, fell between us and the world, I felt, in a way I could not understand, that some singular and unexpected thing was about to happen. I went over to the mantlepiece, and finding that a little chainless bronze censer, set, upon the outside, with pieces of painted china by Orazio Fontana, which I had filled with antique amulets, had fallen upon its side and poured out its contents, I began to gather the amulets into the bowl, partly to collect my thoughts and partly with that habitual reverence which seemed to me the due of things so long connected with secret hopes and fears. 'I see,' said Michael Robartes, 'that you are still fond of incense, and I can show you an incense more precious than any you have ever seen,' and as he spoke he took the censer out of my hand and put the amulets in a little heap between the *athanor* and the *alembic*. I sat down, and he sat down at the side of the fire, and sat there for awhile looking into the fire, and holding the censer in his hand. 'I have come to ask you something,' he said, 'and the incense will fill the room, and our thoughts, with its sweet odour while we are talking. I got it from an old man in Syria, who said it was made from flowers, of one kind with the flowers that laid their heavy purple petals upon the hands and upon the hair and upon the feet of Christ in the Garden of

Gethsemane, and folded Him in their heavy breath, until he cried against the cross and his destiny.' He shook some dust into the censer out of a small silk bag, and set the censer upon the floor and lit the dust which sent up a blue stream of smoke, that spread out over the ceiling, and flowed downwards again until it was like Milton's banyan tree. It filled me, as incense often does, with a faint sleepiness, so that I started when he said, 'I have come to ask you that question which I asked you in Paris, and which you left Paris rather than answer.'

He had turned his eyes towards me, and I saw them glitter in the firelight, and through the incense, as I replied: 'You mean, will I become an initiate of your Order of the Alchemical Rose? I would not consent in Paris, when I was full of unsatisfied desire, and now that I have at last fashioned my life according to my desire, am I likely to consent?'

'You have changed greatly since then,' he answered. 'I have read your books, and now I see you among all these images, and I understand you better than you do yourself, for I have been with many and many dreamers at the same cross—ways. You have shut away the world and gathered the gods about you, and if you do not throw yourself at their feet, you will be always full of lassitude, and of wavering purpose, for a man must forget he is miserable in the bustle and noise of the multitude in this world and in time; or seek a mystical union with the multitude who govern this world and time.' And then he murmured something I could not hear, and as though to someone I could not see.

For a moment the room appeared to darken, as it used to do when he was about to perform some singular experiment, and in the darkness the peacocks upon the doors seemed to glow with a more intense colour. I cast off the illusion, which was, I believe, merely caused by memory, and by the twilight of incense, for I would not acknowledge that he could overcome my now mature intellect; and I said: 'Even if I grant that I need a spiritual belief and some form of worship, why should I go to Eleusis and not to Calvary?' He leaned forward and began speaking with a slightly rhythmical intonation, and as he spoke I had to struggle again with the shadow, as of some older night than the night of the sun, which began to dim the light of the candles and to blot out the little gleams upon the corner of picture− frames and on the bronze divinities, and to turn the blue of the incense to a heavy purple; while it left the peacocks to glimmer and glow as though each separate colour were a living spirit. I had fallen into a profound dream−like reverie in which I heard him speaking as at a distance. 'And yet there is no one who communes with only one god,' he was saying, 'and the more a man lives in imagination and in a refined understanding, the more gods does he meet with and talk with, and the more does he come under the power of Roland, who sounded in the Valley of Roncesvalles the last trumpet of the body's will and pleasure; and of Hamlet, who saw them perishing away, and sighed; and of Faust, who looked for them up and down the world and could not find them; and under the power of all those countless divinities who have taken upon themselves spiritual bodies in the minds of the modern poets and romance writers, and under the power of the old divinities, who since the Renaissance have won everything of their ancient worship except the sacrifice of birds and fishes, the fragrance of garlands and the smoke of incense. The many think humanity made these divinities, and that it can unmake them again; but we who have seen them pass in rattling harness, and in soft robes, and heard them speak with articulate voices while we lay in deathlike trance, know that they are always making and unmaking humanity, which is indeed but the trembling of their lips.'

He had stood up and begun to walk to and fro, and had become in my waking dream a shuttle weaving an immense purple web whose folds had begun to fill the room. The room seemed to have become inexplicably silent, as though all but the web and the weaving were at an end in the world. 'They have come to us; they have come to us,' the voice began again; 'all that have ever been in your reverie, all that you have met with in books. There is Lear, his head still wet with the thunder–storm, and he laughs because you thought yourself an existence who are but a shadow, and him a shadow who is an eternal god; and there is Beatrice, with her lips half parted in a smile, as though all the stars were about to pass away in a sigh of love; and there is the mother of the God of humility who cast so great a spell over men that they have tried to unpeople their hearts that he might reign alone, but she holds in her hand the rose whose every petal is a god; and there, O swiftly she comes! is Aphrodite under a twilight falling from the wings of numberless sparrows, and about her feet are the grey and white doves.' In the midst of my dream I saw him hold out his left arm and pass his right hand over it as though he stroked the wings of doves. I made a violent effort which seemed almost to tear me in two, and said with forced determination: 'You would sweep me away into an indefinite world which fills me with terror; and yet a man is a great man just in so far as he can make his mind reflect everything with indifferent precision like a mirror.' I seemed to be perfectly master of myself, and went on, but more rapidly: 'I command you to leave me at once, for your ideas and phantasies are but the illusions that creep like maggots into civilizations when they begin to decline, and into minds when they begin to decay.' I had grown suddenly angry, and seizing the *alembic* from the table, was about to rise and strike him with it, when the peacocks on the door behind him appeared to grow immense; and then the *alembic* fell from my fingers and I was drowned in a tide of green and blue and bronze feathers, and as I struggled hopelessly I heard a distant voice saying: 'Our master Avicenna has written that all life proceeds out of corruption.' The glittering feathers had now covered me completely, and I knew that I had struggled for hundreds of years, and was conquered at last. I was sinking into the depth when the green and blue and bronze that seemed to fill the world became a sea of flame and swept me away, and as I was swirled along I heard a voice over my head cry, 'The mirror is broken in two pieces,' and another voice answer, 'The mirror is broken in four pieces,' and a more distant voice cry with an exultant cry, 'The mirror is broken into numberless pieces'; and then a multitude of pale hands were reaching towards me, and strange gentle faces bending above me, and half wailing and half caressing voices uttering words that were forgotten the moment they were spoken. I was being lifted out of the tide of flame, and felt my memories, my hopes, my thoughts, my will, everything I held to be myself, melting away; then I seemed to rise through numberless companies of beings who were, I understood, in some way more certain than thought, each wrapped in his eternal moment, in the perfect lifting of an arm, in a little circlet of rhythmical words, in dreaming with dim eyes and half—closed eyelids. And then I passed beyond these forms, which were so beautiful they had almost ceased to be, and, having endured strange moods, melancholy, as it seemed, with the weight of many worlds, I passed into that Death which is Beauty herself, and into that Loneliness which all the multitudes desire without ceasing. All things that had ever lived seemed to come and dwell in my heart, and I in theirs; and I had never again known mortality or tears, had I not suddenly fallen from the certainty of vision into the uncertainty of dream, and become a drop of molten gold falling with immense rapidity, through a night elaborate with stars, and all about me a melancholy exultant wailing. I fell and fell and fell, and then the wailing was but the wailing of the wind in the chimney, and I awoke to find myself leaning upon the table and supporting my head with my hands. I saw the *alembic* swaying from side to side in the distant corner it had rolled to, and Michael Robartes watching me and waiting. 'I will go wherever you will,' I said, 'and do whatever you bid me, for I have been with eternal things.' 'I knew,' he replied, 'you must need answer as you have answered, when I heard the storm begin. You must come to a great distance, for we were commanded to build our temple between the pure multitude by the waves and the impure multitude of men.'

Part III

I did not speak as we drove through the deserted streets, for my mind was curiously empty of familiar thoughts and experiences; it seemed to have been plucked out of the definite world and cast naked upon a shoreless sea. There were moments when the vision appeared on the point of returning, and I would half–remember, with an ecstasy of joy or sorrow, crimes and heroisms, fortunes and misfortunes; or begin to contemplate, with a sudden leaping of the heart, hopes and terrors, desires and ambitions, alien to my orderly and careful life; and then I would awake shuddering at the thought that some great imponderable being had swept through my mind. It was indeed days before this feeling passed perfectly away, and even now, when I have sought refuge in the only definite faith, I feel a great tolerance for those people with incoherent personalities, who gather in the chapels and meeting–places of certain obscure sects, because I also have felt fixed habits and principles dissolving before a power, which was *hysterica passio* or sheer madness, if you will, but was so powerful in its melancholy exultation that I tremble lest it wake again and drive me from my new–found peace.

When we came in the grey light to the great half–empty terminus, it seemed to me I was so changed that I was no more, as man is, a moment shuddering at eternity, but eternity weeping and laughing over a moment; and when we had started and Michael Robartes had fallen asleep, as he soon did, his sleeping face, in which there was no sign of all that had so shaken me and that now kept me wakeful, was to my excited mind more like a mask than a face. The fancy possessed me that the man behind it had dissolved away like salt in water, and that it laughed and sighed, appealed and denounced at the bidding of beings greater or less than man. 'This is not Michael Robartes at all: Michael Robartes is dead; dead for ten, for twenty years perhaps,' I kept repeating to myself. I fell at last into a feverish sleep, waking up from time to time when we rushed past some little town, its slated roofs shining with wet, or still lake gleaming in the cold morning light. I had been too pre—occupied to ask where we were going, or to notice what tickets Michael Robartes had taken, but I knew now from the direction of the sun that we were going westward; and presently I knew also, by the way in which the trees had grown into the semblance of tattered beggars flying with bent heads towards the east, that we were approaching the western coast. Then immediately I saw the sea between the low hills upon the left, its dull grey broken into white patches and lines.

When we left the train we had still, I found, some way to go, and set out, buttoning our coats about us, for the wind was bitter and violent. Michael Robartes was silent, seeming anxious to leave me to my thoughts; and as we walked between the sea and the rocky side of a great promontory, I realized with a new perfection what a shock had been given to all my habits of thought and of feelings, if indeed some mysterious change had not taken place in the substance of my mind, for the grey waves, plumed with scudding foam, had grown part of a teeming, fantastic inner life; and when

Michael Robartes pointed to a square ancient–looking house, with a much smaller and newer building under its lee, set out on the very end of a dilapidated and almost deserted pier, and said it was the Temple of the Alchemical Rose, I was possessed with the phantasy that the sea, which kept covering it with showers of white foam, was claiming it as part of some indefinite and passionate life, which had begun to war upon our orderly and careful days, and was about to plunge the world into a night as obscure as that which followed the downfall of the classical world. One part of my mind mocked this phantastic terror, but the other, the part that still lay half plunged in vision, listened to the clash of unknown armies, and shuddered at unimaginable fanaticisms, that hung in those grey leaping waves.

We had gone but a few paces along the pier when we came upon an old man, who was evidently a watchman, for he sat in an overset barrel, close to a place where masons had been lately working upon a break in the pier, and had in front of him a fire such as one sees slung under tinkers' carts. I saw that he was also a voteen, as the peasants say, for there was a rosary hanging from a nail on the rim of the barrel, and I saw I shuddered, and I did not know why I shuddered. We had passed him a few yards when I heard him cry in Gaelic, 'Idolaters, idolaters, go down to Hell with your witches and your devils; go down to Hell that the herrings may come again into the bay'; and for some moments I could hear him half screaming and half muttering behind us. 'Are you not afraid,' I said, 'that these wild fishing people may do some desperate thing against you?'

'I and mine,' he answered, 'are long past human hurt or help, being incorporate with immortal spirits, and when we die it shall be the consummation of the supreme work. A time will come for these people also, and they will sacrifice a mullet to Artemis, or some other fish to some new divinity, unless indeed their own divinities, the Dagda, with his overflowing cauldron, Lug, with his spear dipped in poppy– juice lest it rush forth hot for battle. Aengus, with the three birds on his shoulder, Bodb and his red swineherd, and all the heroic children of Dana, set up once more their temples of grey stone. Their reign has never ceased, but only waned in power a little, for the Sidhe still pass in every wind, and dance and play at hurley, and fight their sudden battles in every hollow and on every hill; but they cannot build their temples again till there have been martyrdoms and victories, and perhaps even that long–foretold battle in the Valley of the Black Pig.'

Keeping close to the wall that went about the pier on the seaward side, to escape the driving foam and the wind, which threatened every moment to lift us off our feet, we made our way in silence to the door of the square building. Michael Robartes opened it with a key, on which I saw the rust of many salt winds, and led me along a bare passage and up an uncarpeted stair to a little room surrounded with bookshelves. A meal would be brought, but only of fruit, for I must submit to a tempered fast before the ceremony, he explained, and with it a book on the doctrine and method of the Order, over which I was to spend what remained of the winter daylight. He then left me, promising to return an hour before the ceremony. I began searching among the bookshelves, and found one of the most exhaustive alchemical libraries I have ever seen. There were the works of Morienus, who hid his immortal body under a shirt of hair—cloth; of Avicenna, who was a drunkard and yet controlled numberless legions of spirits; of Alfarabi, who put so many spirits into his lute that he could make men laugh, or weep, or fall in deadly trance as he would; of Lully, who transformed himself into the likeness of a red cock; of Flamel, who with his wife Parnella achieved the elixir many hundreds of years ago, and is fabled to live still in Arabia among the Dervishes; and of many of less fame. There were very few mystics but alchemical mystics, and because, I had little doubt, of the devotion to one god of the greater number and of the limited sense of beauty, which Robartes would hold an inevitable consequence; but I did notice a complete set of facsimiles of the prophetical writings of William Blake, and probably because of the multitudes that thronged his illumination and were 'like the gay fishes on the wave when the moon sucks up the dew.' I noted also many poets and prose writers of every age, but only those who were a little weary of life, as indeed the greatest have been everywhere, and who cast their imagination to us, as a something they needed no longer now that they were going up in their fiery chariots.

Presently I heard a tap at the door, and a woman came in and laid a little fruit upon the table. I judged that she had once been handsome, but her cheeks were hollowed by what I would have held, had I seen her anywhere else, an excitement of the flesh and a thirst for pleasure, instead of which it doubtless was an excitement of the imagination and a thirst for beauty. I asked her some question concerning the ceremony, but getting no answer except a shake of the head, saw that I must await initiation in silence. When I had eaten, she came again, and having laid a curiously wrought bronze box on the table, lighted the candles, and took away the plates and the remnants. So soon as I was alone, I turned to the box, and found that the peacocks of Hera spread out their tails over the sides and lid, against a background, on which were wrought great stars, as though to affirm that the heavens were a part of their glory. In the box was a book bound in vellum, and having upon the vellum and in very delicate colours, and in gold, the alchemical rose with many spears thrusting against it, but in vain, as was shown by the shattered points of those nearest to the petals. The book was written upon vellum, and in beautiful clear letters, interspersed with symbolical pictures and illuminations, after the manner of the Splendor Soils.

The first chapter described how six students, of Celtic descent, gave themselves separately to the study of alchemy, and solved, one the mystery of the Pelican, another the mystery of the green Dragon, another the mystery of the Eagle, another that of Salt and Mercury. What seemed a succession of accidents, but was, the book declared, the contrivance of preternatural powers, brought them together in the garden of an inn in the South of France, and while they talked together the thought came to them that alchemy was the gradual distillation of the contents of the soul, until they were ready to put off the mortal and put on the immortal. An owl passed, rustling among the vine—leaves overhead, and then an old woman came, leaning upon a stick, and, sitting close to them, took up the thought where they had dropped it. Having expounded the whole principle of spiritual alchemy, and bid them found the Order of the Alchemical Rose, she passed from among them, and when they would have followed she was nowhere to be seen. They formed themselves into an Order, holding their goods and making their researches in common, and, as they became perfect in the alchemical doctrine, apparitions came and went among them, and taught them more and more marvellous mysteries. The book then went on to expound so much of these as the neophyte was permitted to know, dealing at the outset and at considerable length with the independent reality of our thoughts, which was, it declared, the doctrine from which all true doctrines rose. If you imagine, it said, the semblance of a living being, it is at once possessed by a wandering soul, and goes hither and thither working good or evil, until the moment of its death has come; and gave many examples, received, it said, from many gods. Eros had taught them how to fashion forms in which a divine soul could dwell, and whisper what they would into sleeping minds; and Ate forms from which demonic beings could pour madness, or unquiet dreams, into sleeping blood; and Hermes, that if you powerfully imagined a hound at your bedside it would keep watch there until you woke, and drive away all but the mightiest demons, but that if your imagination was weakly, the hound would be weakly also, and the demons prevail, and the hound soon die; and Aphrodite, that if you made, by a strong imagining, a dove crowned with silver and had it flutter over your head, its soft cooing would make sweet dreams of immortal love gather and brood over mortal sleep; and all divinities alike had revealed with many warnings and lamentations that all minds are continually giving birth to such beings, and sending them forth to work health or disease, joy or madness. If you would give forms to the evil powers, it went on, you were to make them ugly, thrusting out a lip, with the thirsts of life, or breaking the proportions of a body with the burdens of life; but the divine powers would only appear in beautiful shapes, which are but, as it were, shapes trembling out of existence, folding up into a timeless ecstasy, drifting with half—shut eyes, into a sleepy stillness. The bodiless souls who descended into these forms were what men called the moods; and worked all great changes in the world; for just as the magician or the artist could call them when he would, so they could call out of the mind of the magician or the artist, or if they were demons, out of the mind of the mad or the ignoble, what shape they would, and through its voice and its gestures pour themselves out upon the world. In this way all great events were accomplished; a mood, a divinity, or a demon, first descending like a faint sigh into men's minds and then changing their thoughts and their actions until hair that was yellow had grown black, or hair that was black had grown yellow, and empires moved their border, as though they were but drifts of leaves. The rest of the book contained symbols of form, and sound, and colour, and their attribution to divinities and demons, so that the initiate might fashion a shape for any divinity or any demon, and be as powerful as Avicenna among those who live under the roots of tears and of laughter.

Part IV

A couple of hours after Sunset Michael Robartes returned and told me that I would have to learn the steps of an exceedingly antique dance, because before my initiation could be perfected I had to join three times in a magical dance, for rhythm was the wheel of Eternity, on which alone the transient and accidental could be broken, and the spirit set free. I found that the steps, which were simple enough, resembled certain antique Greek dances, and having been a good dancer in my youth and the master of many curious Gaelic steps, I soon had them in my memory. He then robed me and himself in a costume which suggested by its shape both Greece and Egypt, but by its crimson colour a more passionate life than theirs; and having put into my hands a little chainless censer of bronze, wrought into the likeness of a rose, by some modern craftsman, he told me to open a small door opposite to the door by which I had entered. I put my hand to the handle, but the moment I did so the fumes of the incense, helped perhaps by his mysterious glamour, made me fall again into a dream, in which I seemed to be a mask, lying on the counter of a little Eastern shop. Many persons, with eyes so bright and still that I knew them for more than human, came in and tried me on their faces, but at last flung me into a corner with a little laughter; but all this passed in a moment, for when I awoke my hand was still upon the handle. I opened the door, and found myself in a marvellous passage, along whose sides were many divinities wrought in a mosaic, not less beautiful than the mosaic in the Baptistery at

Ravenna, but of a less severe beauty; the predominant colour of each divinity, which was surely a symbolic colour, being repeated in the lamps that hung from the ceiling, a curiously–scented lamp before every divinity. I passed on, marvelling exceedingly how these enthusiasts could have created all this beauty in so remote a place, and half persuaded to believe in a material alchemy, by the sight of so much hidden wealth; the censer filling the air, as I passed, with smoke of ever–changing colour.

I stopped before a door, on whose bronze panels were wrought great waves in whose shadow were faint suggestions of terrible faces. Those beyond it seemed to have heard our steps, for a voice cried: 'Is the work of the Incorruptible Fire at an end?' and immediately Michael Robartes answered: 'The perfect gold has come from the *atbanor* .' The door swung open, and we were in a great circular room, and among men and women who were dancing slowly in crimson robes. Upon the ceiling was an immense rose wrought in mosaic; and about the walls, also in mosaic, was a battle of gods and angels, the gods glimmering like rubies and sapphires, and the angels of the one greyness, because, as Michael Robartes whispered, they had renounced their divinity, and turned from the unfolding of their separate hearts, out of love for a God of humility and sorrow. Pillars supported the roof and made a kind of circular cloister, each pillar being a column of confused shapes, divinities, it seemed, of the wind, who rose as in a whirling dance of more than human vehemence, and playing upon pipes and cymbals; and from among these shapes were thrust out hands, and in these hands were censers. I was bid place my censer also in a hand and take my place and dance, and as I turned from the pillars towards the dancers, I saw that the floor was of a green stone, and that a pale Christ on a pale cross was wrought in the midst. I asked Robartes the meaning of this, and was told that they desired 'To trouble His unity with their multitudinous feet.' The dance wound in and out, tracing upon the floor the shapes of petals that copied the petals in the rose overhead, and to the sound of hidden instruments which were perhaps of an antique pattern, for I have never heard the like; and every moment the dance was more passionate, until all the winds of the world seemed to have awakened under our feet. After a little I had grown weary, and stood under a pillar watching the coming and going of those flame—like figures; until gradually I sank into a half—dream, from which I was awakened by seeing the petals of the great rose, which had no longer the look of mosaic, falling slowly through the incense—heavy air, and, as they fell, shaping into the likeness of living beings of an extraordinary beauty. Still faint and cloud—like, they began to dance, and as they danced took a more and more definite shape, so that I was able to distinguish beautiful Grecian faces and august Egyptian faces, and now and again to name a divinity by the staff in his hand or by a bird fluttering over his head; and soon every mortal foot danced by the white foot of an immortal; and in the troubled eyes that looked into untroubled shadowy eyes, I saw the brightness of uttermost desire as though they had found at length, after unreckonable wandering, the lost love of their youth. Sometimes, but only for a moment, I saw a faint solitary figure with a Rosa veiled face, and carrying a faint torch, flit among the dancers, but like a dream within a dream, like a shadow of a shadow, and I knew by an understanding born from a deeper fountain than thought, that it was Eros himself, and that his face was veiled because no man or woman from the beginning of the world has ever known what love is, or looked into his eyes, for Eros alone of divinities is altogether a spirit, and hides in passions not of his essence if he would commune with a mortal heart. So that if a man love nobly he knows love through infinite pity, unspeakable trust, unending sympathy; and if ignobly through vehement jealousy, sudden hatred, and unappeasable desire; but unveiled love he never knows. While I thought these things, a voice cried to me from the crimson figures: 'Into the dance! there is none that can be spared out of the dance; into the dance! into the dance! that the gods may make them bodies out of the substance of our hearts'; and before I could answer, a mysterious wave of passion, that seemed like the soul of the dance moving within our souls, took hold of me, and I was swept, neither consenting nor refusing, into the midst. I was dancing with an immortal august woman, who had black lilies in her hair, and her dreamy gesture seemed laden with a wisdom more profound than the darkness that is between star and star, and with a love like the love that breathed upon the waters; and as we danced on and on, the incense drifted over us and round us, covering us away as in the heart of the world, and ages seemed to pass, and tempests to awake and perish in the folds of our robes and in her heavy hair.

Suddenly I remembered that her eyelids had never quivered, and that her lilies had not dropped a black petal, or shaken from their places, and understood with a great horror that I danced with one who was more or less than human, and who was drinking up my soul as an ox drinks up a wayside pool; and I fell, and darkness passed over me.

Part V

I awoke suddenly as though something had awakened me, and saw that I was lying on a roughly painted floor, and that on the ceiling, which was at no great distance, was a roughly painted rose, and about me on the walls half−finished paintings. The pillars and the censers had gone; and near me a score of sleepers lay wrapped in disordered robes, their upturned faces looking to my imagination like hollow masks; and a chill dawn was shining down upon them from a long window I had not noticed before; and outside the sea roared. I saw Michael Robartes lying at a little distance and beside him an overset bowl of wrought bronze which looked as though it had once held incense. As I sat thus, I heard a sudden tumult of angry men and women's voices mix with the roaring of the sea; and leaping to my feet, I went quickly to Michael Robartes, and tried to shake him out of his sleep. I then seized him by the shoulder and tried to lift him, but he fell backwards, and sighed faintly; and the voices became louder and angrier; and there was a sound of heavy blows upon the door, which opened on to the pier. Suddenly I heard a sound of rending wood, and I knew it had begun to give, and I ran to the door of the room. I pushed it open and came out upon a passage whose bare boards clattered under my feet, and found in the passage another door which led into an empty kitchen; and as I passed through the door I heard two crashes in quick succession, and knew by the sudden noise of feet and the shouts that the door which opened on to the pier had fallen inwards. I ran from the kitchen and out into a small yard, and from this down some steps which descended the seaward and sloping side of the pier, and from the steps clambered along the water's edge, with the angry voices ringing in my ears. This part of the pier had been but lately refaced with blocks of granite, so that it was almost clear of seaweed; but when I came to the old part, I found it so slippery with green weed that I had to climb up on to the roadway. I looked towards the Temple of the Alchemical Rose, where the fishermen and the women were still shouting, but somewhat more faintly, and saw that there was no one about the door or upon the pier; but as I looked, a little crowd hurried out of the door and began gathering large stones from where they were heaped up in readiness for the next time a storm shattered the pier, when they would be laid under blocks of granite. While I stood watching the crowd, an old man, who was, I think, the voteen, pointed to me, and screamed out something, and the crowd whitened, for all the faces had turned towards me. I ran, and it was well for me that pullers of the oar are poorer men with their feet than with their arms and their bodies; and yet while I ran I scarcely heard the following feet or the angry voices, for many voices of exultation and lamentation, which were forgotten as a dream is forgotten the moment they were heard, seemed to be ringing in the air over my head.

There are moments even now when I seem to hear those voices of exultation and lamentation, and when the indefinite world, which has but half lost its mastery over my heart and my intellect, seems about to claim a perfect mastery; but I carry the rosary about my neck, and when I hear, or seem to hear them, I press it to my heart and say: 'He whose name is Legion is at our doors deceiving our intellects with subtlety and flattering our hearts with beauty, and we have no trust but in Thee'; and then the war that rages within me at other times is still, and I am at peace.

THE TABLES OF LAW

Part I

'Will you permit me, Aherne,' I said, 'to ask you a question, which I have wanted to ask you for years, and have not asked because we have grown nearly strangers? Why did you refuse the biretta, and almost at the last moment? When you and I lived together, you cared neither for wine, women, nor money, and had thoughts for nothing but theology and mysticism.' I had watched through dinner for a moment to put my question, and ventured now, because he had thrown off a little of the reserve and indifference which, ever since his last return from Italy, had taken the place of our once close friendship. He had just questioned me, too, about certain private and almost sacred things, and my frankness had earned, I thought, a like frankness from him.

When I began to speak he was lifting a glass of that wine which he could choose so well and valued so little; and while I spoke, he set it slowly and meditatively upon the table and held it there, its deep red light dyeing his long delicate fingers. The impression of his face and form, as they were then, is still vivid with me, and is inseparable from another and fanciful impression: the impression of a man holding a flame in his naked hand. He was to me, at that moment, the supreme type of our race, which, when it has risen above, or is sunken below, the formalisms of half-education and the rationalisms of conventional affirmation and denial, turns away, unless my hopes for the world and for the Church have made me blind, from practicable desires and intuitions towards desires so unbounded that no human vessel can contain them, intuitions so immaterial that their sudden and far-off fire leaves heavy darkness about hand and foot. He had the nature, which is half monk, half soldier of fortune, and must needs turn action into dreaming, and dreaming into action; and for such there is no order, no finality, no contentment in this world. When he and I had been students in Paris, we had belonged to a little group which devoted itself to speculations about alchemy and mysticism. More orthodox in most of his beliefs than Michael Robartes, he had surpassed him in a fanciful hatred of all life, and this hatred had found expression in the curious paradox—half borrowed from some fanatical monk, half invented by himself—that the beautiful arts were sent into the world to overthrow nations, and finally life herself, by sowing everywhere unlimited desires, like torches thrown into a burning city. This idea was not at the time, I believe, more than a paradox, a plume of the pride of youth; and it was only after his return to Ireland that he endured the fermentation of belief which is coming upon our people with the reawakening of their imaginative life.

Presently he stood up, saying, 'Come, and I will show you why; you at any rate will understand,' and taking candles from the table, he lit the way into the long paved passage that led to his private chapel. We passed between the portraits of the Jesuits and priests—some of no little fame—his family had given to the Church; and engravings and photographs of pictures that had especially moved him; and the few paintings his small fortune, eked out by an almost penurious abstinence from the things most men desire, had enabled him to buy in his travels. The photographs and engravings were from the masterpieces of many schools; but in all the beauty, whether it was a beauty of religion, of love, or of some fantastical vision of mountain and wood, was the beauty achieved by temperaments which seek always an absolute emotion, and which have their most continual, though not most perfect, expression in the legends and vigils and music of the Celtic peoples. The certitude of a fierce or gracious fervour in the enraptured faces of the angels of Francesca, and in the august faces of the sibyls of Michaelangelo; and the incertitude, as of souls trembling between the excitement of the spirit and the excitement of the flesh, in wavering faces from frescoes in the churches of Siena, and in the faces like thin flames, imagined by the modern symbolists and Pre-Raphaelites, had often made that long, grey, dim, empty, echoing passage become to my eyes a vestibule of eternity.

Almost every detail of the chapel, which we entered by a narrow Gothic door, whose threshold had been worn smooth by the secret worshippers of the penal times, was vivid in my memory; for it was in this chapel that I had first, and when but a boy, been moved by the mediaevalism which is now, I think, the governing influence in my life. The only thing that seemed new was a square bronze box which stood upon the altar before the six unlighted candles and the ebony crucifix, and was like those made in ancient times of more precious substances to hold the sacred books. Aherne made me sit down on an oak bench, and having bowed very low before the crucifix, took the bronze box from the altar, and sat down beside me with the box upon his knees.

'You will perhaps have forgotten,' he said, 'most of what you have read about Joachim of Flora, for he is little more than a name to even the well-read. He was an abbot in Cortale in the twelfth century, and is best known for his prophecy, in a book called *Expositio in Apocalypsin*, that the Kingdom of the Father was past, the Kingdom of the Son passing, the Kingdom of the Spirit yet to come. The Kingdom of the Spirit was to be a complete triumph of the Spirit, the *spiritualis intelligentia* he called it, over the dead letter. He had many followers among the more extreme Franciscans, and these were accused of possessing a secret book of his called the *Liber inducens in Evangelium aeternum*. Again and again groups of visionaries were accused of possessing this terrible book, in which the freedom of the Renaissance lay hidden, until at last Pope Alexander IV. had it found and cast into the flames. I have here the greatest treasure the world contains. I have a copy of that book; and see what great artists have made the robes in which it is wrapped. This bronze box was made by Benvenuto Cellini, who covered it with gods and demons, whose eyes are closed to signify an absorption in the inner light.' He lifted the lid and took out a book bound in leather, covered with filigree work of tarnished silver. 'And this cover was bound by one of the binders that bound for Canevari; while Giulio Clovio, an artist of the later Renaissance, whose work is soft and gentle, took out the beginning page of every chapter of the old copy, and set in its place a page surmounted by an elaborate letter and a miniature of some one of the great whose example was cited in the chapter; and wherever the writing left a little space elsewhere, he put some delicate emblem or intricate pattern.

I took the book in my hands and began turning over the gilded, many-coloured pages, holding it close to the candle to discover the texture of the paper.

'Where did you get this amazing book?' I said. 'If genuine, and I cannot judge by this light, you have discovered one of the most precious things in the world.'

'It is certainly genuine,' he replied. 'When the original was destroyed, one copy alone remained, and was in the hands of a lute- player of Florence, and from him it passed to his son, and so from generation to generation until it came to the lute-player who was father to Benvenuto Cellini, and from him it passed to Giulio Clovio, and from Giulio Clovio to a Roman engraver; and then from generation to generation, the story of its wandering passing on with it, until it came into the possession of the family of Aretino, and so Giulio Aretino, an artist and worker in metals, and student of the cabbalistic reveries of Pico della Mirandola. He spent many nights with me at Rome, discussing philosophy; and at last I won his confidence so perfectly that he showed me this, his greatest treasure; and, finding how much I valued it, and feeling that he himself was growing old and beyond the help of its teaching, he sold it to me for no great sum, considering its great preciousness.

'What is the doctrine?' I said. 'Some mediaeval straw-splitting about the nature of the Trinity, which is only useful to-day to show how many things are unimportant to us, which once shook the world?'

'I could never make you understand,' he said with a sigh, 'that nothing is unimportant in belief, but even you will admit that this book goes to the heart. Do you see the tables on which the commandments were written in Latin?' I looked to the end of the room, opposite to the altar, and saw that the two marble tablets were gone, and that two large empty tablets of ivory, like large copies of the little tablets we set over our desks, had taken their place. 'It has swept the commandments of the Father away,' he went on, 'and displaced the commandments of the Son by the commandments of the Holy Spirit. The first book is called *Fractura Tabularum*. In the first chapter it mentions the names of the great artists who made them graven things and the likeness of many things, and adored them and served them; and the second the names of the great wits who took the name of the Lord their God in vain; and that long third chapter, set with the emblems of sanctified faces, and having wings upon its borders, is the praise of breakers of the seventh day and wasters of the six days, who yet lived comely and pleasant days. Those two chapters tell of men and women who railed upon their parents, remembering that their god was older than the god of their parents; and that which has the sword of Michael for an emblem commends the kings that wrought secret murder and so won for their people a peace that was *amore somnoque gravata et vestibus versicoloribus*, "heavy with love and sleep and many- coloured raiment"; and that with the pale star at the closing has the lives of the noble

46

youths who loved the wives of others and were transformed into memories, which have transformed many poorer hearts into sweet flames; and that with the winged head is the history of the robbers who lived upon the sea or in the desert, lives which it compares to the twittering of the string of a bow, *nervi stridentis instar*, and those two last, that are fire and gold, and devoted to the satirists who bore false witness against their neighbours and yet illustrated eternal wrath, and to those that have coveted more than other men the house of God, and all things that are His, which no man has seen and handled, except in madness and in dreams.

'The second book is called *Lex Secreta*, and describes the true inspiration of action, the only Eternal Evangel; and ends with a vision, which he saw among the mountains of La Sila, of his disciples sitting throned in the blue deep of the air, and laughing aloud, with a laughter that was like the rustling of the wings of Time: *Cœlis in cœruleis ridentes sedebant discipuli mei super thronos: talis erat risus, qualis temporis pennati susurrus.*'

'I know little of Joachim of Flora,' I said, 'except that Dante set him in Paradise among the great doctors. If he held a heresy so singular, I cannot understand how no rumours of it came to the ears of Dante; and Dante made no peace with the enemies of the Church.'

'Joachim of Flora acknowledged openly the authority of the Church, and even asked that all his published writings, and those to be published by his desire after his death, should be submitted to the censorship of the Pope. He considered that those whose work was to live and not to reveal were children and that the Pope was their father; but he taught in secret that certain others, and in always increasing numbers, were elected, not to live, but to reveal that hidden substance of God which is colour and music and softness and a sweet odour; and that these have no father but the Holy Spirit. Just as poets and painters and musicians labour at their works, building them with lawless and lawful things alike, so long as they embody the beauty that is beyond the grave, these children of the Holy Spirit labour at their moments with eyes upon the shining substance on which Time has heaped the refuse of creation; for the world only exists to be a tale in the ears of coming generations; and terror and content, birth and death, love and hatred, and the fruit of the Tree, are but instruments for that supreme art which is to win us from life and gather us into eternity like doves into their dove-cots.

'I shall go away in a little while and travel into many lands, that I may know all accidents and destinies, and when I return, will write my secret law upon those ivory tablets, just as poets and romance- writers have written the principles of their art in prefaces; and will gather pupils about me that they may discover their law in the study of my law, and the Kingdom of the Holy Spirit be more widely and firmly established.'

He was pacing up and down, and I listened to the fervour of his words and watched the excitement of his gestures with not a little concern. I had been accustomed to welcome the most singular speculations, and had always found them as harmless as the Persian cat, who half closes her meditative eyes and stretches out her long claws, before my fire. But now I would battle in the interests of orthodoxy, even of the commonplace; and yet could find nothing better to say than: 'It is not necessary to judge every one by the law, for we have also Christ's commandment of love.'

He turned and said, looking at me with shining eyes: 'Jonathan Swift made a soul for the gentlemen of this city by hating his neighbour as himself.'

'At any rate, you cannot deny that to teach so dangerous a doctrine is to accept a terrible responsibility.'

'Leonardo da Vinci,' he replied, 'has this noble sentence: "The hope and desire of returning home to one's former state is like the moth's desire for the light; and the man who with constant longing awaits each new month and new year, deeming that the things he longs for are ever too late in coming, does not perceive that he is longing for his own destruction." How then can the pathway which will lead us into the heart of God be other than dangerous? Why should you, who are no materialist, cherish the continuity and order of the world as those do who have only the world? You do not value the writers who will express nothing unless their reason understands how it will make what is called the right more easy; why, then, will you deny a like freedom to the supreme art, the art which is the foundation of all arts? Yes, I shall send out of this chapel saints, lovers, rebels, and prophets: souls that will surround themselves with peace, as with a nest made with grass; and others over whom I shall weep. The dust shall fall for many years over this little box;

and then I shall open it; and the tumults which are, perhaps, the flames of the Last Day shall come from under the lid.'

I did not reason with him that night, because his excitement was great and I feared to make him angry; and when I called at his house a few days later, he was gone and his house was locked up and empty. I have deeply regretted my failure both to combat his heresy and to test the genuineness of his strange book. Since my conversion I have indeed done penance for an error which I was only able to measure after some years.

Part II

I was walking along one of the Dublin quays, on the side nearest the river, about ten years after our conversation, stopping from time to time to turn over the works upon an old bookstall, and thinking, curiously enough, of the terrible destiny of Michael Robartes, and his brotherhood, when I saw a tall and bent man walking slowly along the other side of the quay. I recognised, with a start, in a lifeless mask with dim eyes, the once resolute and delicate face of Owen Aherne. I crossed the quay quickly, but had not gone many yards before he turned away, as though he had seen me, and hurried down a side street; I followed, but only to lose him among the intricate streets on the north side of the river. During the next few weeks I inquired of everybody who had once known him, but he had made himself known to nobody; and I knocked, without result, at the door of his old house; and had nearly persuaded myself that I was mistaken, when I saw him again in a narrow street behind the Four Courts, and followed him to the door of his house.

I laid my hand on his arm; he turned quite without surprise; and indeed it is possible that to him, whose inner life had soaked up the outer life, a parting of years was a parting from forenoon to afternoon. He stood holding the door half open, as though he would keep me from entering; and would perhaps have parted from me without further words had I not said: 'Owen Aherne, you trusted me once, will you not trust me again, and tell me what has come of the ideas we discussed in this house ten years ago?—but perhaps you have already forgotten them.'

'You have a right to hear,' he said, 'for since I have told you the ideas, I should tell you the extreme danger they contain, or rather the boundless wickedness they contain; but when you have heard this we must part, and part for ever, because I am lost, and must be hidden!'

I followed him through the paved passage, and saw that its corners were choked with dust and cobwebs; and that the pictures were grey with dust and shrouded with cobwebs; and that the dust and cobwebs which covered the ruby and sapphire of the saints on the window had made it very dim. He pointed to where the ivory tablets glimmered faintly in the dimness, and I saw that they were covered with small writing, and went up to them and began to read the writing. It was in Latin, and was an elaborate casuistry, illustrated with many examples, but whether from his own life or from the lives of others I do not know. I had read but a few sentences when I imagined that a faint perfume had begun to fill the room, and turning round asked Owen Aherne if he were lighting the incense.

'No,' he replied, and pointed where the thurible lay rusty and empty on one of the benches; as he spoke the faint perfume seemed to vanish, and I was persuaded I had imagined it.

'Has the philosophy of the *Liber inducens in Evangelium aeternum* made you very unhappy?' I said.

'At first I was full of happiness,' he replied, 'for I felt a divine ecstasy, an immortal fire in every passion, in every hope, in every desire, in every dream; and I saw, in the shadows under leaves, in the hollow waters, in the eyes of men and women, its image, as in a mirror; and it was as though I was about to touch the Heart of God. Then all changed and I was full of misery; and in my misery it was revealed to me that man can only come to that Heart through the sense of separation from it which we call sin, and I understood that I could not sin, because I had discovered the law of my being, and could only express or fail to express my being, and I understood that God has made a simple and an arbitrary law that we may sin and repent!'

He had sat down on one of the wooden benches and now became silent, his bowed head and hanging arms and listless body having more of dejection than any image I have met with in life or in any art. I went and stood leaning against the altar, and watched him, not knowing what I should say; and I noticed his black closely- buttoned coat, his short hair, and shaven head, which preserved a memory of his priestly ambition, and understood how Catholicism had seized him in the midst of the vertigo he called philosophy; and I noticed his lightless eyes and his earth-coloured complexion, and understood how she had failed to do more than hold him on the margin: and I was full of an anguish of pity.

'It may be,' he went on, 'that the angels who have hearts of the Divine Ecstasy, and bodies of the Divine Intellect, need nothing but a thirst for the immortal element, in hope, in desire, in dreams; but we whose hearts perish every moment, and whose bodies melt away like a sigh, must bow and obey!'

I went nearer to him and said, 'Prayer and repentance will make you like other men.'

'No, no,' he said, 'I am not among those for whom Christ died, and this is why I must be hidden. I have a leprosy that even eternity cannot cure. I have seen the whole, and how can I come again to believe that a part is the whole? I have lost my soul because I have looked out of the eyes of the angels.'

Suddenly I saw, or imagined that I saw, the room darken, and faint figures robed in purple, and lifting faint torches with arms that gleamed like silver, bending above Owen Aherne; and I saw, or imagined that I saw, drops, as of burning gum, fall from the torches, and a heavy purple smoke, as of incense, come pouring from the flames and sweeping about us. Owen Aherne, more happy than I who have been half initiated into the Order of the Alchemical Rose, or protected perhaps by his great piety, had sunk again into dejection and listlessness, and saw none of these things; but my knees shook under me, for the purple-robed figures were less faint every moment, and now I could hear the hissing of the gum in the torches. They did not appear to see me, for their eyes were upon Owen Aherne; now and again I could hear them sigh as though with sorrow for his sorrow, and presently I heard words which I could not understand except that they were words of sorrow, and sweet as though immortal was talking to immortal. Then one of them waved her torch, and all the torches waved, and for a moment it was as though some great bird made of flames had fluttered its plumage, and a voice cried as from far up in the air, 'He has charged even his angels with folly, and they also bow and obey; but let your heart mingle with our hearts, which are wrought of Divine Ecstasy, and your body with our bodies, which are wrought of Divine Intellect.' And at that cry I understood that the Order of the Alchemical Rose was not of this earth, and that it was still seeking over this earth for whatever souls it could gather within its glittering net; and when all the faces turned towards me, and I saw the mild eyes and the unshaken eyelids, I was full of terror, and thought they were about to fling their torches upon me, so that all I held dear, all that bound me to spiritual and social order, would be burnt up, and my soul left naked and shivering among the winds that blow from beyond this world and from beyond the stars; and then a voice cried, 'Why do you fly from our torches that were made out of the trees under which Christ wept in the Garden of Gethsemane? Why do you fly from our torches that were made out of sweet wood, after it had perished from the world?'

It was not until the door of the house had closed behind my flight, and the noise of the street was breaking on my ears, that I came back to myself and to a little of my courage; and I have never dared to pass the house of Owen Aherne from that day, even though I believe him to have been driven into some distant country by the spirits whose name is legion, and whose throne is in the indefinite abyss, and whom he obeys and cannot see.

THE ADORATION OF THE MAGI

I was sitting reading late into the night a little after my last meeting with Aherne, when I heard a light knocking on my front door; and found upon the doorstep three very old men with stout sticks in their hands, who said they had been told I would be up and about, and that they were to tell me important things. I brought them into my study, and when the peacock curtains had closed behind us, I set their chairs for them close to the fire, for I saw that the frost was on their great-coats of frieze and upon the long beards that flowed almost to their waists. They took off their great-coats, and leaned over the fire warming their hands, and I saw that their clothes had much of the country of our time, but a little also, as it seemed to me, of the town life of a more courtly time. When they had warmed themselves—and they warmed themselves, I thought, less because of the cold of the night than because of a pleasure in warmth for the sake of warmth— they turned towards me, so that the light of the lamp fell full upon their weather-beaten faces, and told the story I am about to tell. Now one talked and now another, and they often interrupted one another, with a desire, like that of countrymen, when they tell a story, to leave no detail untold. When they had finished they made me take notes of whatever conversation they had quoted, so that I might have the exact words, and got up to go, and when I asked them where they were going, and what they were doing, and by what names I should call them, they would tell me nothing, except that they had been commanded to travel over Ireland continually, and upon foot and at night, that they might live close to the stones and the trees and at the hours when the Immortals are awake.

I have let some years go by before writing out this story, for I am always in dread of the illusions which come of that inquietude of the veil of the Temple, which M. Mallarmé considers a characteristic of our times; and only write it now because I have grown to believe that there is no dangerous idea which does not become less dangerous when written out in sincere and careful English.

The three old men were three brothers, who had lived in one of the western islands from their early manhood, and had cared all their lives for nothing except for those classical writers and old Gaelic writers who expounded an heroic and simple life. Night after night in winter, Gaelic story-tellers would chant old poems to them over the poteen; and night after night in summer, when the Gaelic story-tellers were at work in the fields or away at the fishing, they would read to one another Virgil and Homer, for they would not enjoy in solitude, but as the ancients enjoyed. At last a man, who told them he was Michael Robartes, came to them in a fishing-boat, like Saint Brendan drawn by some vision and called by some voice; and told them of the coming again of the gods and the ancient things; and their hearts, which had never endured the body and pressure of our time, but only of distant times, found nothing unlikely in anything he told them, but accepted all simply and were happy. Years passed, and one day, when the oldest of the old men, who had travelled in his youth and thought sometimes of other lands, looked out on the grey waters, on which the people see the dim outline of the Islands of the Young—the Happy Islands where the Gaelic heroes live the lives of Homer's Phaeacians—a voice came out of the air over the waters and told him of the death of Michael Robartes. While they were still mourning, the next oldest of the old men fell asleep whilst he was reading out the Fifth Eclogue of Virgil, and a strange voice spoke through him, and bid them set out for Paris, where a dying woman would give them secret names of the gods, which can be perfectly spoken only when the mind is steeped in certain colours and certain sounds and certain odours; but at whose perfect speaking the immortals cease to be cries and shadows, and walk and talk with one like men and women.

They left their island, and were at first troubled at all they saw in the world, and came to Paris, and there the youngest met a person in a dream, who told him they were to wander about at hazard until those who had been guiding their footsteps had brought them to a street and a house, whose likeness was shown him in the dream. They wandered hither and thither for many days, until one morning they came into some narrow and shabby streets, on the south of the Seine, where women with pale faces and untidy hair looked at them out of the windows; and just as they were about to turn back because Wisdom could not have alighted in so foolish a neighbourhood, they came to the street and the house of the dream. The oldest of the old men, who still remembered some of the modern languages he had known in his youth, went up to the door and knocked, and when he had knocked, the next in age to him said it was not a good house, and could not be the house they were looking for, and urged him to ask for somebody who could not be there and go away. The door was opened by an old over-dressed woman, who said, 'O, you are her three kinsmen from Ireland. She has been expecting you all day.' The old men looked at one another and followed her upstairs, passing doors from which pale and untidy women thrust out their heads, and into a room where a beautiful woman lay asleep, another woman sitting by her.

The old woman said, 'Yes, they have come at last; now she will be able to die in peace,' and went out.

'We have been deceived by devils,' said one of the old men, 'for the Immortals would not speak through a woman like this.'

'Yes,' said another, 'we have been deceived by devils, and we must go away quickly.'

'Yes,' said the third, 'we have been deceived by devils, but let us kneel down for a little, for we are by the death-bed of one that has been beautiful.' They knelt down, and the woman sitting by the bed whispered, and as though overcome with fear, and with lowered head, 'At the moment when you knocked she was suddenly convulsed and cried out as I have heard a woman in childbirth and fell backward as though in a swoon. Then they watched for a little the face upon the pillow and wondered at its look, as of unquenchable desire, and at the porcelain-like refinement of the vessel in which so malevolent a flame had burned.

Suddenly the second oldest of them crowed like a cock, till the room seemed to shake with the crowing. The woman in the bed still slept on in her death-like sleep, but the woman who sat by her head crossed herself and grew pale, and the youngest of the old men cried out, 'A devil has gone into him, and we must be-gone or it will go into us also.' Before they could rise from their knees, a resonant chanting voice came from the lips that had crowed and said:— 'I am not a devil, but I am Hermes the Shepherd of the Dead, I run upon the errands of the gods, and you have heard my sign, that has been my sign from the old days. Bow down before her from whose lips the secret names of the immortals, and of the things near their hearts, are about to come, that the immortals may come again into the world. Bow down, and understand that when they are about to overthrow the things that are to-day and bring the things that were yesterday, they have no one to help them, but one whom the things that are to- day have cast out. Bow down and very low, for they have chosen for their priestess this woman in whose heart all follies have gathered, and in whose body all desires have awaked; this woman who has been driven out of Time, and has lain upon the bosom of Eternity. After you have bowed down the old things shall be again, and another Argo shall carry heroes over sea, and another Achilles beleaguer another Troy.'

The voice ended with a sigh, and immediately the old man awoke out of sleep, and said, 'Has a voice spoken through me, as it did when I fell asleep over my Virgil, or have I only been asleep?'

The oldest of them said, 'A voice has spoken through you. Where has your soul been while the voice was speaking through you?'

'I do not know where my soul has been, but I dreamed I was under the roof of a manger, and I looked down and I saw an ox and an ass; and I saw a red cock perching on the hay-rack; and a woman hugging a child; and three old men in chain armour kneeling with their heads bowed very low in front of the woman and the child. While I was looking the cock crowed and a man with wings on his heels swept up through the air, and as he passed me, cried out, "Foolish old men, you had once all the wisdom of the stars." I do not understand my dream or what it would have us do, but you who have heard the voice out of the wisdom of my sleep know what we have to do.'

Then the oldest of the old men told him they were to take the parchments they had brought with them out of their pockets and spread them on the ground. When they had spread them on the ground, they took out of their pockets their pens, made of three feathers which had fallen from the wing of the old eagle that is believed to have talked of wisdom with Saint Patrick.

'He meant, I think,' said the youngest, as he put their ink- bottles by the side of the rolls of parchment, 'that when people are good the world likes them and takes possession of them, and so eternity comes through people who are not good or who have been forgotten. Perhaps Christianity was good and the world liked it, so now it is going away and the Immortals are beginning to awake.'

'What you say has no wisdom,' said the oldest, 'because if there are many Immortals, there cannot be only one Immortal.'

Then the woman in the bed sat up and looked about her with wild eyes; and the oldest of the old men said: 'Lady, we have come to write down the secret names,' and at his words a look of great joy came into her face. Presently she began to speak slowly, and yet eagerly, as though she knew she had but a little while to live, and in the Gaelic of their own country; and she spoke to them many secret powerful names, and of the colours, and odours, and weapons, and instruments of music and instruments of handicraft belonging to the owners of those names; but most about the Sidhe of Ireland and of their love for the Cauldron, and the Whetstone, and the Sword, and the Spear. Then she tossed feebly for a while and moaned, and when she spoke again it was in so faint a murmur that the woman who sat by the bed leaned down to listen, and while she was listening the spirit went out of the body.

The oldest of the old men said in French, 'There must have been yet one name which she had not given us, for she murmured a name while the spirit was going out of the body,' and the woman said, 'She was merely murmuring over the name of a symbolist painter she was fond of. He used to go to something he called the Black Mass, and it was he who taught her to see visions and to hear voices. She met him for the first time a few months ago, and we have had no peace from that day because of her talk about visions and about voices. Why! it was only last night that I dreamed I saw a man with a red beard and red hair, and dressed in red, standing by my bedside. He held a rose in one hand, and tore it in pieces with the other hand, and the petals drifted about the room, and became beautiful people who began to dance slowly. When I woke up I was all in a heat with terror.'

This is all the old men told me, and when I think of their speech and of their silence, of their coming and of their going, I am almost persuaded that had I followed them out of the house, I would have found no footsteps on the snow. They may, for all I or any man can say, have been themselves Immortals: immortal demons, come to put an untrue story into my mind for some purpose I do not understand. Whatever they were, I have turned into a pathway which will lead me from them and from the Order of the Alchemical Rose. I no longer live an elaborate and haughty life, but seek to lose myself among the prayers and the sorrows of the multitude. I pray best in poor chapels, where frieze coats brush against me as I kneel, and when I pray against the demons I repeat a prayer which was made I know not how many centuries ago to help some poor Gaelic man or woman who had suffered with a suffering like mine:—

Seacht b-páidreacha fó seacht
Chuir Muire faoi n-a Mac,
Chuir Brighid faoi n-a brat,
Chuir Dia faoi n-a neart,

Eidir sinn 'san Sluagh Sidhe,
Eidir sinn 'san Sluagh Gaoith.

Seven paters seven times,
Send Mary by her Son,
Send Bridget by her mantle,
Send God by His strength,
Between us and the faery host,
Between us and the demons of the air.

www.ingramcontent.com/pod-product-compliance
Lightning Source LLC
Chambersburg PA
CBHW031134260626
47153CB00021B/1470